8 / 00

W9-BYW-941

~~Milton Free Public Library~~
~~P.O. Box 19, 104 Main St.~~
~~Milton, Maine 04239~~

CUSHING LIBRARY
PO Box 25
Cushing, ME 04563

DONALD J. SOBOL

ENCYCLOPEDIA BROWN SETS THE PACE

Illustrations by Ib Ohlsson

Wilton Free Public Library
P.O. Box 454 104 Main St.
Wilton, Maine 04294

Four Winds Press   New York

Other Encyclopedia Brown titles by Donald J. Sobol

Encyclopedia Brown, Boy Detective
Encyclopedia Brown and the Case of the Secret Pitch
Encyclopedia Brown Finds the Clues
Encyclopedia Brown Gets His Man
Encyclopedia Brown Solves Them All
Encyclopedia Brown Keeps the Peace
Encyclopedia Brown Saves the Day
Encyclopedia Brown Tracks Them Down
Encyclopedia Brown Shows the Way
Encyclopedia Brown Takes the Case
Encyclopedia Brown Lends a Hand
Encyclopedia Brown and the Case of the Dead Eagles
Encyclopedia Brown and the Case of the Midnight Visitor
Encyclopedia Brown's Record Book
of Weird and Wonderful Facts
Encyclopedia Brown Carries On
Encyclopedia Brown's Second Record Book
of Weird and Wonderful Facts
Encyclopedia Brown Takes the Cake:
A Cook and Case Book

For Mary Guilbert Brand

Text copyright © 1982 by Donald J. Sobol
Illustrations copyright © 1982 by Scholastic Inc.
All rights reserved. No part of this book may be reproduced or transmitted
in any form or by any means, electronic or mechanical, including
photocopying, recording, or by any information storage and retrieval
system, without permission in writing from the Publisher.

Four Winds Press
Macmillan Publishing Company
866 Third Avenue, New York, NY 10022
Collier Macmillan Canada, Inc.

Printed in the United States of America

10   9   8   7   6

Library of Congress Cataloging in Publication Data
Sobol, Donald J. [date]
Encyclopedia Brown sets the pace.
Summary: More mysterious cases for "America's
Sherlock Holmes in sneakers" to solve for the standard
twenty-five cent fee. Solutions are included at the
back of the book.
[I. Mystery and detective stories.] I. Title.
PZ7.S68524Ert   [Fic]   81-69511
ISBN 0-02-786200-3   AACR

CONTENTS

THE CASE OF THE SUPERMARKET SHOPPER

IN EVERY CITY AND TOWN ACROSS America, crime was a serious problem. Except in Idaville.

There the forces of law and order were in control. Crooks knew better than to try anything. If they did, they were certain to be caught. No one, child or grownup, got away with breaking the law in Idaville.

How did Idaville do it?

Only three persons knew, and they weren't telling.

Apart from doing in crooks, Idaville was like most seaside towns. It had lovely beaches, three movie theaters, and two delicatessens. It had churches, a synagogue, and four banks.

The chief of police was Mr. Brown. People called him a genius, but he knew better.

True, he was an excellent police chief, and his officers were honest and brave. But the *real* genius behind the town's war on crime was Chief Brown's only child, ten-year-old Encyclopedia—America's Sherlock Holmes in sneakers.

Whenever Chief Brown came up against a mystery he could not solve, he took the proper action. He drove home. At the dinner table, he went over the facts with Encyclopedia. Before dessert, Encyclopedia had the case solved.

Chief Brown wanted the President to proclaim Encyclopedia a national resource. He hated keeping his son undercover. But whom could he tell?

Who would believe him?

Who would believe that the mastermind behind Idaville's amazing police record was still outgrowing his pants?

So Chief Brown said not a word to anyone, and neither, of course, did Mrs. Brown.

For his part, Encyclopedia never mentioned

the help he gave his father. He didn't want to seem better than other fifth graders.

But there was nothing he could do about his nickname. No one except his parents and his teachers called him by his real name, Leroy. Everyone else called him Encyclopedia.

An encyclopedia is a book or set of books filled with facts from *A* to *Z*. So was Encyclopedia's head. He had read more books than anyone in Idaville. His pals claimed he was more fun than a library. They could take him on fishing trips.

At the dinner table Saturday evening, Chief Brown picked at his roast beef. Encyclopedia and his mother waited. They knew the sign. A case had him baffled.

At last Chief Brown put down his fork. "A painting by Ignazio Saracco was stolen Friday night from the home of William Quinn."

Encyclopedia let out a whistle. Ignazio Saracco was a minor fifteenth-century artist. Even so, any painting by him was worth thousands of dollars today.

"Why not go over the case with Leroy, dear?" Mrs. Brown suggested quietly. "He's never failed you."

Chief Brown sighed heavily. "All right, but I don't have a single clue." He put down his

3

fork and told Encyclopedia everything he had learned about the theft of the painting.

Mr. Quinn lived in a small house on Suncrest Drive. The Saracco painting had hung over the fireplace for twenty years. Friday morning Mrs. Quinn had left for Glenn City to visit her mother, leaving Mr. Quinn alone. In the afternoon, he had invited three friends—Edgar Trad, Tom Houser, and Murray Finkelstein—to come over and play checkers.

They played for three hours. Then, at six o'clock, Mr. Quinn called a halt. He had to go to Morey's Supermarket on Clearview Avenue, a five-minute drive away. His wife had asked him to buy four rolls of paper towels before she returned home.

"I've shopped at that supermarket," Mrs. Brown interrupted. "It's so hard to pay, unless you use the speed checkout counter. But then you must have no more than ten purchases."

"I remember your complaining about the crowds," said Chief Brown. "You quit shopping there because the lines at the five regular checkout counters were so long."

"They ought to put in two more speed counters," Mrs. Brown said wistfully.

Chief Brown nodded sympathetically and went on with the case.

Mr. Quinn's three friends had asked him to

4

buy small items for them while he was at the supermarket. Mr. Finkelstein wanted two loaves of rye bread, Mr. Houser wanted four tubes of Gladbrim toothpaste, and Mr. Trad wanted a brown whisk broom.

Mr. Quinn agreed to shop for them. Since they lived on the same block, it was no bother.

"While he was at the supermarket, one of the three might have sneaked back into the house," said Mrs. Brown.

"Possibly," replied Chief Brown. "The house was empty for an hour. The back door had been forced and the painting was missing when he returned from the supermarket."

"Do his friends have alibis?" Mrs. Brown asked.

"Each of them can account for his time while Mr. Quinn was shopping," answered Chief Brown. "Mr. Finkelstein said he was alone in his garage repairing a rake. Mr. Houser said he was in his backyard tending his flowers. Mr. Trad said he spent about an hour reading in his study. None of them, however, has a witness."

"Then one of them must be the thief," asserted Mrs. Brown. "They were the only ones who knew that Mr. Quinn was at the supermarket!"

"Not so," Chief Brown replied. "Any num-

ber of people may have noticed Mr. Quinn driving from his house. And others who knew him might have seen him at the supermarket."

Chief Brown leaned back in his chair. "Besides," he continued, "Mr. Quinn told me that he greeted two friends by the soup shelves. They were Winnie Dowling, who lives next door, and Clyde Dennison, who lives two blocks away. Put them on the list of suspects."

"But don't forget, dear," said Mrs. Brown, "only Mr. Trad, Mr. Finkelstein, and Mr. Houser knew that Mrs. Quinn was in Glenn City for the day. Only they knew that the house would be empty while Mr. Quinn shopped."

"Not so, again," disagreed Chief Brown. "Mrs. Quinn goes to visit her mother every Friday morning. She always returns about the same hour, ten o'clock at night. I expect many people are familiar with her trips."

"Then anyone in the neighborhood could be the thief," Mrs. Brown said hopelessly.

"And anyone who was in the supermarket Friday evening," added Chief Brown.

Mrs. Brown seemed ready to give up. She looked at Encyclopedia for help. With so little to work on, could he solve the mystery?

The boy detective had closed his eyes. He

always closed his eyes when he did his deepest thinking.

Suddenly his eyes opened. He asked one question. Usually he needed but one question to solve the most puzzling case.

"In what order, Dad, did the three friends ask Mr. Quinn to shop for them at the supermarket?"

Chief Brown drew a small notebook from his breast pocket. He flipped the pages. "Here it is. . . . Mr. Trad asked first, then Mr. Finkelstein, and then Mr. Houser."

Never before had Mrs. Brown appeared disappointed in Encyclopedia's question. She was disappointed now, however.

"How can the order be important, Leroy?" she asked. "You can't accuse one of the three men because he wanted Mr. Quinn to do a bit of shopping for him. Why, I shop for friends frequently."

"But no one robbed our house, Mom," replied Encyclopedia. "The key to the theft of the painting is what Mr. Quinn did at the supermarket."

Chief Brown leaned forward in his chair, suddenly alert and interested.

"Leroy," he said, "if I had a suspect . . . I could put a round-the-clock tail on him. He'd be bound to lead us to the painting sooner or later."

"He wouldn't have had time to sell the painting," said Encyclopedia. "It's probably still in his house."

"For heaven's sake, Leroy, who is it?" exclaimed Mrs. Brown.

Encyclopedia finished buttering a roll. "The house to search belongs to—"

WHO WAS THE THIEF?

(Turn to page 80 for the solution to "The Case of the Supermarket Shopper.")

THE CASE OF THE DINOSAUR HUNTER

THROUGHOUT THE YEAR, ENCYCLO-pedia solved cases for his father at the dinner table. During the summer, he helped the children of the neighborhood, as well.

When school let out, he opened a detective agency in the garage. Every morning he hung out his sign.

BROWN DETECTIVE AGENCY
13 Rover Avenue
Leroy Brown, President
No Case Too Small
25¢ Per Day Plus Expenses

The first customer on Monday was Garth Pouncey. He was seven.

"Have you seen any dinosaurs around here?" he asked.

"Not for sixty-five million years," replied Encyclopedia.

Garth's face fell. "I think Bugs Meany put one over on me," he said.

"Oh, no. Not Bugs again," Encyclopedia said, groaning.

Bugs Meany was the leader of a gang of tough older boys. They called themselves the Tigers. They should have called themselves the Razors. They were always getting into scrapes.

Garth said, "If there are no dinosaurs around, then this dinosaur-hunting license Bugs sold me is as phony as pig feathers."

He handed Encyclopedia an important-looking sheet with a drawing of a Tyrannosaurus and a lot of words.

Encyclopedia read: " 'SPECIAL PERMIT. This license entitles the holder to pursue, shoot, kill, and remove any of the following dinosaurs.' " The dinosaurs that could be hunted lawfully were listed in two columns.

"Bugs said I could hunt one dinosaur from column A and three from column B, unless

12

they were with young," Garth said. "I'd have to clean a dead dinosaur within four days and have it approved by him."

"He told you he was Idaville's game warden for dinosaurs," guessed Encyclopedia.

Garth nodded. "You sure know Bugs."

"I've had to stop his fast deals before," Encyclopedia said. He tapped the sheet. "You can get one of these fun licenses for nothing by writing to a place in Utah."

Garth wailed. "I promised to pay Bugs three dollars for it on Monday!" He laid twenty-five cents on the gasoline can beside the detective. "Can I hire you to get me out of this mess?"

"Tell me how you got into it," Encyclopedia said.

Garth explained. Three hours ago he had biked to Mill Pond to swim. As he crossed the little bridge there, his front wheel struck a rut, and he tumbled against Bugs.

"Bugs's towel dropped into the water, and he got awful mad," Garth said. "So I lent him my towel for the day."

"Nice thinking," approved Encyclopedia.

"Bugs said I was so nice that he'd do me a big favor," said Garth. "He'd sell me a dinosaur-hunting license, and I could pay him on Monday. I grabbed the license and lit out before he changed his mind and pitched me after his towel."

"I'll take the case," Encyclopedia said. "I think I can talk Bugs into forgetting about the three dollars. The license is an out-and-out gyp."

"Get back my towel, too," Garth urged. "I pulled it from the dryer as Mom was unloading the machine this morning. If I tell Mom I lost it, she'll have a fit."

The Tigers' clubhouse was an unused toolshed behind Mr. Sweeney's Auto Body Shop. As Encyclopedia approached with Garth, he saw a towel hanging from a branch near the front door.

"That looks like my towel," Garth said. "What if Bugs won't return it?"

"We'll have to prove it's yours," Encyclopedia replied.

Garth moaned. "How? It's a plain white towel."

Their voices brought Bugs to the door of the clubhouse. "You should wear a hat," he growled at Encyclopedia, "so I know that strange growth on your neck is your head."

The detective was used to Bugs's warm and friendly greetings. "We've come to return your worthless dinosaur-hunting license and get back Garth's towel," he said.

"Take your mouth south," snapped Bugs. "This little kid owes me three dollars. The license doesn't guarantee big game, just the right to hunt. And the towel *stays*."

Garth bit his thumbnail nervously.

Bugs sneered at him. "I've got a cure for fingernail biters." He held up a fist. "I knock out their teeth."

"Time to leave," whispered Garth. "I'd like to avoid unnecessary surgery."

"Not until Bugs agrees to take back the license and return your towel," insisted Encyclopedia.

"That's *my* towel," Bugs declared. "It fell into Mill Pond this morning, and I hung it out to dry. I never even had a chance to use it."

"Garth bumped your towel into the pond by accident," Encyclopedia said. "A lot of kids must have seen it happen."

Bugs's lips moved in a cocky grin.

Garth said lamely, "No one else was around but two of his Tigers. . . . Wait! There were some soap flakes on top of Mom's dryer. There may be some in the towel!"

Encyclopedia felt the soft, fluffy white towel, searching for soap flakes. There were none.

Bugs's grin widened. "Go on, Mr. Brains,

prove that isn't my towel. I'll take back the hunting license, and he can have the towel. If you can't prove it, I'm going to start dealing out lumps!"

"Save the tough-guy talk, Bugs," Encyclopedia advised. "I can prove you're lying."

HOW?

(Turn to page 81 for the solution to "The Case of the Dinosaur Hunter.")

THE CASE OF THE USED FIRECRACKERS

BUGS MEANY'S HEART BEAT WITH A great desire. It was to get even with Encyclopedia.

Bugs hated being outsmarted all the time. He longed to help the boy detective turn things over in his mind by knocking him head over heels.

But Bugs never threw a punch. Whenever he felt the urge, he remembered Sally Kimball.

Sally was the prettiest girl in the fifth

grade and the best athlete. Moreover, she had proved she could tame the toughest Tiger!

When they had fought last, Sally had put knuckle-dents in Bugs's hide. She had left him lying on his back, stunned and moaning, "Deal the cards."

Since Sally joined the Brown Detective Agency as a junior partner, Bugs had quit trying to rough up Encyclopedia. He continued to plan his revenge, however—on both of them.

"You'd better watch out for Bugs," Encyclopedia warned Sally. "He hates you as much as he hates me."

Sally agreed. "If Bugs were voted the Man of the Hour, we'd still have to watch him every minute."

"Speaking of time, we're due out at the old cattle range in thirty minutes," Encyclopedia said.

As they biked to the range, Encyclopedia spoke about the mysterious telephone call he had received last night.

"The caller said to meet him at the range at ten this morning—by the third telephone pole from the left side of the road," Encyclopedia said. "He hinted that the case was important and he'd pay extra."

"Didn't he say what the case was about?" asked Sally.

"He said he'd tell us when we got there."

"Strange. . . . Did you recognize his voice?"

"No," answered Encyclopedia. "It sounded like he was putting on a fake accent. We'll just have to be careful."

The old cattle range was five hundred acres of unused land. There was nothing on it but a row of telephone poles, trees, underbrush, snakes, and birds.

Encyclopedia and Sally left the paved road. They followed a dirt one that wandered this way and that, its destination lost in the wilderness. After several hundred yards, it turned under the telephone wires.

The detectives leaned their bikes against a palmetto palm. The third telephone pole on their left stood in a small clearing.

"There's no one here," Sally said uneasily.

"Not quite," remarked Encyclopedia. He pointed to the telephone wires. About a dozen small gray birds were perched directly above them.

Sally had stooped over and was picking up something from the ground. "A used firecracker," she said with surprise. She looked around. "The clearing is covered with them."

21

"There must be a few hundred," Encyclopedia observed.

"Let's go," Sally suggested. "Now."

"Too late," replied Encyclopedia.

A police car was coming down the dirt road. It stopped beside their bikes. After a minute, Officer Friedman got out and walked up to the detectives.

A bush behind Encyclopedia rustled. Bugs Meany came leaping into the clearing. "Did you hear it?" he asked Officer Friedman. "Did you hear it?"

Officer Friedman shot Bugs a questioning glance.

"They exploded a firecracker just as you drove up," cried Bugs. "You must have been giving your position over the radio."

"I was," admitted Officer Friedman. "So I could have missed hearing a firecracker explode."

"What's this all about?" demanded Encyclopedia.

"Oooh, listen to him, will you?" howled Bugs. "Mr. Goody-Good has finally been caught with the goods! He can't lie his way out of this. Him and Miss Muscles have been setting off firecrackers here all summer."

"The station received a call this morning,"

22

Officer Friedman said. "The complaint was that a boy and girl have been exploding firecrackers here and were planning to do it again at ten o'clock this morning."

Bugs drew himself up straight as an Eagle Scout. "Fireworks are dangerous and against the law," he announced.

Sally whirled on him. "What are *you* doing here?"

"I made the call to the police," Bugs boasted. "Us Tigers uphold the law. Why, one firecracker could set this field blazing. Five hundred acres of natural beauty up in smoke, *pfft!* All because of a couple of smart-aleck lawbreakers."

"That's a lie, you teen-age junk heap!" snapped Sally.

"I've got news for you," snarled Bugs. "If looks were a crime, you'd have been born in prison."

"Don't get smart," Sally retorted. "It will clash with your brains."

"Easy does it, you two," Officer Friedman said. He peered at the litter of burned firecrackers. "I'll have to report this."

Encyclopedia protested. He told Officer Friedman about the telephone call summoning them to the clearing. The policeman con-

tinued writing in his notebook.

"We didn't do anything," insisted Sally. "Bugs is trying to get us into trouble."

"My, how she blabbers on. Pitiful," said Bugs. "Think of the headlines tomorrow: 'Idaville Disgraced—Son of Police Chief and Female Sidekick Nabbed in the Act!'"

Sally's cheeks reddened in helpless rage. She looked up at the birds perched on the telephone wires. "They saw everything. If only birds could talk!"

"They don't have to say a word," remarked Encyclopedia. "As usual, Bugs talked too much."

WHAT WAS BUGS'S MISTAKE?

(Turn to page 82 for the solution to "The Case of the Used Firecrackers.")

THE CASE OF THE UGLIEST DOG

ENCYCLOPEDIA AND SALLY REACHED the high school shortly before the First Annual Idaville Children's Dog Show was to start.

Little kids and dogs of every description were gathered at one end of the football field. Sally stooped to pet a cocker spaniel wearing sunglasses and a straw hat.

"Hold it!" called Scott Curtis, clicking his camera.

Scott was the neighborhood shutterbug.

He could make a photograph of a drowning bullfrog look like the centerfold of a dance magazine.

"That was a nifty shot," he said to Sally. "I'm the official show photographer, you know."

"Gosh, Scott, how neat!" Sally exclaimed.

"Thanks," Scott replied. "This is a great day for me and all animal lovers."

"So I see," Encyclopedia commented. "But aren't there an awful lot of strange mutts here?"

"That's the idea," Scott said. "Any dog can be entered. This isn't one of those snobby shows."

"Why the costumes?" asked Sally.

"There's a class for the best-dressed dog," Scott answered. "There are other classes for the funniest dog, the oldest-looking dog, and the ugliest dog. The main event is worst in show."

Scott pointed to Jim Mack and his dog, Twitchy. "Twitchy is the favorite to win ugliest dog," he said.

Encyclopedia could see why. Twitchy looked like a cross between a St. Bernard and a French rat.

"I guess every little kid should be proud of

his pet," Sally said softly.

"Any pet is beautiful," stated Scott. "It's just that some aren't so beautiful on the outside."

He turned to snap a picture of a passing collie in an apron, beads, and wig. Then he waved to the detectives and hurried off to take more pictures.

Encyclopedia and Sally wandered among the dogs. Most of them looked like they had been given a home out of sympathy.

At noon the judging started. For each class there was a champion and ten runners-up. Nearly every kid would win a prize.

Twitchy didn't win anything. When the ugliest-dog contest was called, she was fast asleep and could not be wakened. Unable to make it to the judges' ring, she was disqualified.

Despite the excitement over Twitchy, the show went on.

Kate Felton's pooch, Something Else, won ugliest dog and later worst in show, but only after Kate had convinced the judges that Something Else was a dog, not a dust mop.

After the prizes had been awarded, Scott Curtis collected the champions and runners-up for a group photograph. He asked Kate Felton, the grand winner, to pose in the center

of the front row. She refused.

She had tripped, she said, against the freshly painted side of the gym. The front of her skirt was smeared with dried white paint. "I look awful," she wailed.

The others argued with her in vain. Sally offered to exchange skirts for the picture.

"Oh, no! I can't have my picture taken in your purple polka-dot skirt and my orange blouse," Kate complained. "The colors are gross together."

The other children lost patience.

"Aw, hurry up and change, Kate," screamed Bill Seiple.

"Who'll notice the colors, anyway?" yelled Ted Corbin.

"They won't even show," chimed in Earl Hanes.

"Stop acting like a spoiled brat," scolded Debbie Worthheimer.

"Oh, all right," said Kate, and reluctantly joined the group.

That evening, Sally stayed at Encyclopedia's house for dinner. She was still grumbling about Kate Felton's behavior when the telephone rang. It was Jim Mack, Twitchy's owner.

"My dad took Twitchy to the veterinarian,"

he told Encyclopedia. "Twitchy was drugged!"

Half an hour later Scott Curtis rang the doorbell. "Somebody changed the film in my camera," he said. "The film I just developed has only the four shots I snapped of the winners. It's black and white, and everyone knows I was shooting color."

He explained that he had left his camera in the custodian's office for half an hour while he paraded his dog, Brownie, in the ugliest-dog class. During that time, Mr. Everet, the custodian, had gone outside, leaving the office empty for about ten minutes.

"If someone wanted your film, why didn't he steal the camera?" Sally mused.

"Probably he didn't dare risk being seen with it," said Scott. "But why didn't he just steal the film? Why did he replace it with another roll?"

"Because," said Encyclopedia thoughtfully, "he didn't want you to learn that anything was wrong while he was still at the show."

Sally said, "One thing is certain. The guilty person must be someone who had a camera of his own at the show."

"That's no help," Scott objected. "Almost everyone had a camera. What puzzles me is why anyone wanted *my* film."

"Perhaps you took a picture of something you weren't supposed to," suggested Encyclopedia.

Scott shook his head. "I photographed only dogs and people."

"Kate Felton is the one," declared Sally. "All that fuss about paint on her clothes. Encyclopedia, you should question her!"

"No need to," replied the boy detective. "I already know who drugged Twitchy and stole Scott's film."

WHO?

(Turn to page 83 for the solution to "The Case of the Ugliest Dog.")

THE CASE OF HILBERT'S SONG

ON WEDNESDAY AFTERNOON, ENCY-clopedia and Sally closed the detective agency at one o'clock and headed for Maggie DeLong's birthday party.

At the corner of Bleeker Street, Hilbert Capps joined them without a word.

Hilbert was the state junior hollering champion. Normally he was quick to talk about his hobby. How hollering was a dying art. How hollerers were being replaced by screechers, screamers, and yellers. But not today.

He greeted the detectives with a friendly wave and fell into step beside them. He did not holler a single chorus of "Precious Memories," his medal-winning selection.

"You're unusually quiet, Hilbert," commented Sally after they had walked a block in silence.

"My top notes are shot," said Hilbert in a voice raspy enough to smooth asparagus tips. "I overdid it yesterday."

"You joined a protest march?" inquired Encyclopedia.

"Naw, I shouted down two hound dogs, a garbage-pail lid, and a washboard," replied Hilbert.

He explained. Three days ago, he had passed Maggie DeLong's house and heard some men and women screaming.

"I thought a person was getting murdered," Hilbert said. "Turned out it was just the television. An announcer came on and said, 'You have just heard the top song of the month, "Stompin' in Mother Hubbard's Slippers." ' "

"I'll bet you were glad to learn the screaming was a song and not a murder," Sally said. "It must have eased your mind."

"It *made up* my mind," corrected Hilbert. "Right then I decided to earn some big money. If that was a hit song, I knew I could write a better one and sell it to a record company."

Yesterday, he said, Maggie DeLong had lent him her tape recorder. They set it on a table in her backyard. He brought over his neighbor's two hound dogs, a metal garbage-pail lid, a washboard, and two sticks.

"I beat on the lid and scraped the washboard and hollered at the top of my lungs," Hilbert said. "In no time the dogs started to howl. The more I beat and scraped and hollered, the louder they barked and howled. When the tape was completed, I felt real proud of myself."

"Hoppin' harmonies!" exclaimed Encyclopedia. "You may have the smash tune of the year. What do you call it?"

Hilbert said, " 'I've Been Crying Over You Since You Fell Into the Well.' You'll hear the tape today. Maggie promised to play it at her birthday party."

At Maggie's house, the three children left their gifts on the hall table. Then they joined the other guests in the living room.

After an hour of games, Hilbert's great moment arrived. Maggie clapped her hands for silence.

"I have a surprise," she announced. "Hilbert has recorded an original song. I want to play it for you. It's super!"

The children settled down, uncertain of

what to expect. Maggie went to the back of the house. She was gone several minutes.

When she reappeared, she looked terribly upset. A single tear, running from the outside corner of her eye, glistened on her cheek. She wiped it with a pink handkerchief and blew her nose.

"H-Hilbert!" she gasped, "the tape is missing!"

The children were shocked. Sally was the first to speak. "You probably just misplaced it."

Maggie shook her head. "No, I'm certain I left it on my desk."

"We'll organize a search," Sally said.

While the other children looked about the living room, Encyclopedia, Sally, and Hilbert went with Maggie to her bedroom.

"I put the tape and recorder here," Maggie said, rapping her desk top. "They were here when the first guest arrived."

Sally shooed away Maggie's gray cat, Ladybird, and picked up the empty recorder. "If the thief took only the tape, he must have believed Hilbert's song was very valuable. Who else knew about the song?"

"I didn't tell a soul," Maggie said.

"The only ones I told were my folks and

you and Encyclopedia," Hilbert said.

"The neighbors must have heard us make the recording," Maggie said. "Some of their kids are here at the party."

"You can't accuse them," Hilbert objected. "Everyone in the neighborhood must have heard me and those hound dogs."

"But Charlotte Bevins and Mitch Waller live close enough to have *seen* what you were doing," Sally said.

Hilbert brightened. "We could frisk Charlotte and Mitch," he said. "They haven't had a chance to hide the tape anyplace."

"Wrong," Maggie said glumly. "All the kids went outdoors during the scavenger hunt."

Sally frowned. "Just before I went outside, Mitch passed me. He said he was going to the kitchen to see if your mom needed help."

"Mitch is tone deaf," said Maggie. "He couldn't tell a hit tune from an alarm clock ringing."

"Hang on," Hilbert said. "Charlotte excused herself just before the scavenger hunt. She said she had to fix her hair."

"Charlotte fixes her hair every hour," said Maggie. "To tell the truth, I doubt if either Charlotte or Mitch is the thief. You might as well blame my cat."

40

Sally grumbled, "We're no place." She turned to Encyclopedia impatiently. "Don't you have *any* idea who stole the tape?"

"Of course I have," answered the detective.

WHO WAS THE THIEF?

(Turn to page 84 for the solution to "The Case of Hilbert's Song.")

THE CASE OF THE CROWING ROOSTER

THURSDAY EVENING ENCYCLOPEDIA was trimming the bushes in front of his house when Lisa Periwinkle raced by on her bicycle.

"What's the hurry, Lisa?" called the detective.

"I'm on my way to make my fortune," Lisa hollered. She skidded to a halt and regarded Encyclopedia with interest. "Aren't you going, too?"

"Where?"

"The city dump," answered Lisa. "Wilford

Wiggins called a meeting there for seven thirty. He has a big deal just for us kids."

"The lazy con artist," mumbled Encyclopedia.

Wilford Wiggins was a high school dropout who began his day by going back to sleep. In the afternoon he figured ways of fast-talking the neighborhood children out of their savings.

"Wilford didn't tell me about the meeting," Encyclopedia observed.

"He's sore at you," Lisa replied. "You always squelch his big money-making deals. Frankly, sometimes I don't trust him myself."

"You can never trust Wilford," Encyclopedia said. "He might be telling the truth."

Lisa's face showed uncertainty. "He promised to make us kids so much money we'd be rolling in it," she said.

"Wilford's an expert in rolling," Encyclopedia said. "He has to stuff his mattress with golf balls to roll out of bed."

"Then come to the dump," Lisa urged. "You might keep me and the other kids from losing our money."

"I suppose I'd better go along," Encyclopedia said. "I'll get my bike. Won't be a second."

It was just seven thirty when they arrived at the city dump. The first shades of sunset were beginning to close in.

Wilford stood facing the crowd of children. Beside him was a youth of about eighteen who wore an overcoat with a bulge in it.

Wilford flung up one hand and then the other, as if to prove he was on the up-and-up.

"Gather round, friends," he called. "That's it, step closer. I don't want you to miss hearing how you can"—he chuckled mysteriously— "feather your nest."

The children murmured with excitement and inched closer. Bugs Meany and two of his Tigers elbowed their way to the front.

Wilford said, "Allow me to introduce my partner, Bill Canfield."

The youth beside Wilford bowed. He drew a rooster from under his overcoat and set it on the ground. Then he took a tiny box from his pocket. The box had two knobs.

Wilford cried, "You're thinking, 'What does this tiny box do?' I'll tell you, my friends. It controls roosters. It's Bill's secret ray!"

"I'll make the rooster crow by sending rays to its brain," Bill announced. He turned the knobs on the tiny box.

The rooster stretched its neck and crowed. It crowed twice more within a minute.

Bill turned the knobs back and tucked the rooster into his overcoat.

"I could make this rooster crow hundreds

45

of times in an hour," he proclaimed. "But I don't want to wear out the poor bird in a mere demonstration."

Wilford was fairly dancing with glee. "You saw Bill do it! You saw his box send out secret rays that made the rooster crow three times!"

"You're full of baloney," jeered Bugs. "That's a trained rooster."

"You can't *train* a rooster, friend," Wilford asserted. "The rays made him crow."

"So what?" cried Bugs. "What's Bill going to invent next? An electric spoon?"

"Bugs is right," Lisa whispered to Encyclopedia. "What good is a ray that makes a rooster crow?"

"I'm sure Wilford has something else up his sleeve," answered Encyclopedia.

Wilford's eyes were gleaming. He had played his audience to a fine pitch of doubt. Now he was ready to turn the doubt into belief.

"Bill is developing a ray to control hens," he declared. "Hens are smarter than roosters. So the hen ray takes longer to work out."

"Hens don't crow," shouted Lisa. "They cluck."

"How right you are!" Wilford trumpeted. "Hens cluck . . . and they lay eggs. Bill is perfecting a ray to make hens lay eggs on command!"

The children suddenly grew still.

"I'm on the brink of success," Bill declared. "But I've run out of money to complete the research. So my pal Wilford called this meeting to give all his young friends a chance to buy a share of my hen ray. With your help, I'll finish the project, and you'll reap the rewards."

"An ordinary hen lays about three hundred eggs a year," Wilford said. "Using the ray, a person can make a hen lay two or three or even ten times that number!"

The children understood what that would mean. Farmers all over America—all over the world—would buy the ray. Starvation would be a thing of the past. And everyone would make a bundle of money.

"Don't miss out," Wilford called. "Step right up. Buy a share in Bill's invention for only five dollars. A year from now you'll thank me with every breath you take."

"I have ten dollars with me," Lisa said to Encyclopedia. "Should I buy two shares?"

"You'd be buying two shares of nothing," replied the detective.

WHY WASN'T ENCYCLOPEDIA FOOLED?

(Turn to page 85 for the solution to "The Case of the Crowing Rooster.")

48

THE CASE
OF THE
BUBBLE GUM
SHOOTOUT

ENCYCLOPEDIA AND SALLY WERE strolling through South Park when they chanced upon Cephas Keefer.

Encyclopedia liked Cephas, though the little fourth grader had a temper like gunpowder. When it exploded, he would do battle with anyone. Usually he overmatched himself.

At the moment, Cephas lay all alone in the shade of a banyan tree. He appeared to be giving himself mouth-to-mouth resuscitation.

His cheeks were puffing and unpuffing, his lips were puckering and unpuckering, and he was making noises like a wounded hippopotamus.

"Oh, dear," Sally said anxiously. "I think he's been punched out again." She hurried to Cephas and asked, "Who did it?"

"Nobody," Cephas answered calmly. He puffed a final puff. "I'm just warming up the old lips."

"For what?" inquired Encyclopedia. "To go three rounds with an air hose?"

"Uh-uh," said Cephas. "I've got a bubble gum shootout with Malcolm Nesbit at noon." He glanced at his wristwatch and jumped to his feet. "I better hurry."

A bubble gum shootout did not happen every day in Idaville, and so the detectives went along. Cephas, who strutted with confidence, explained how the shootout had come about.

It had begun a year ago at a baseball game. Cephas and Malcolm were in the outfield. They chased a long fly ball into some bushes and found a beautiful ten-speed bicycle hidden there.

When the two boys were unable to find the owner, they took the bike to the police station. Officer Carlson told them that if no one claimed the bike in a year, it was theirs. The year had ended yesterday, and the bike was still unclaimed.

"I guess I've been bragging too much about what a great bubble gum blower I am," confessed Cephas. "Malcolm said he could pick anyone—even a perfect stranger—and put him against me. That made me boiling mad. I dared him to try."

"If you defeat the stranger, the bike is yours?" asked Sally.

"Yup," Cephas replied. "And if I lose, the bike is Malcolm's. But I'll win. I'm made for bubble gum. I have the lungs of a lion, the tongue of a cobra, and—"

"The temper of a jackass," Sally said. "Be thankful Encyclopedia is here to keep you from being cheated. Malcolm is tricky. He likes to eat his cake and have yours, too."

At the west end of the park, Malcolm was waiting. He greeted Cephas and smiled coolly at the detectives.

"Now I'll choose your opponent from among perfect strangers," he said to Cephas.

He ambled a hundred feet to a brick path and spoke with several passersby. Encyclopedia could not hear what was said. The passersby laughed, shook their heads, and strolled on.

After many minutes, Malcolm brought back

a blonde girl of about fifteen.

"Meet our volunteer, Teresa Byrnes," he said.

"This is far out, wild," Teresa said. "I haven't blown bubble gum in years."

She set the brown paper bag she had been carrying carefully on the ground. "My lunch," she remarked offhandedly.

Malcolm handed Cephas and Teresa three pieces of gum each. While he went over the rules, Encyclopedia and Sally edged close to the brown paper bag.

"What's inside?" Sally whispered.

Encyclopedia peered in. "A small jar of peanut butter with a screw-on top," he answered, "and a package of paper napkins."

The shootout consisted of three events. "Whoever wins two is the victor," Malcolm declared. He gave Sally a tape measure and grandly appointed her the judge.

The opening event was to blow a bubble while somersaulting. Cephas went first and blew a four-incher.

Teresa applauded and refused her turn. "No, thanks," she protested with a laugh. "I'd break my neck."

After only one bubble, Cephas was halfway to winning the bicycle!

The second event was to blow two or more bubbles at once. Cephas failed on his first attempt. So did Teresa.

On his second attempt, Cephas got out two small bubbles. Suddenly Teresa was all business. She worked the gum in her mouth deliberately, unhurriedly—and blew three bubbles.

"Wow!" she bellowed. "What luck! What luck!"

It was one victory apiece.

The third and deciding event was blowing for size.

Cephas had lost a little of his confidence. He did not glance at Teresa as he took a deep breath and gathered himself together.

A thin tip of pink appeared between his lips and grew steadily into a bubble. It grew and grew until it hid his face. Gently, as if it were a ball of hammered lace, he pulled the bubble free and held it for Sally to measure. Twelve inches!

"I don't know how I did it," he gasped. "I never blew one that big before, and I had a head wind."

Teresa seemed doomed to defeat. Yet she did not look worried. She chewed her gum slowly and worked it against her front teeth.

She took her time.

The bubble appeared, growing faster than Cephas's had. It seemed ready to burst at any second. Then all at once the huge pink beauty was in her hand.

Sally measured it. Twelve and a half inches!

Malcolm grinned triumphantly at Cephas. "A perfect stranger beat you," he crowed. "The bike is mine."

"It is not," said Encyclopedia. "You cheated."

HOW?

(Turn to page 86 for the solution to "The Case of the Bubble Gum Shootout.")

THE CASE
OF THE
BOY JUGGLER

EXCITEMENT HAD GRIPPED ENCY-clopedia's neighborhood for weeks. Talent scouts for a new television program, *Young America*, were coming to Idaville to hold tryouts!

One of Encyclopedia's closest pals, Fangs Liverright, had been practicing an act in secret. He refused to talk about it. He would say only that he did "jaw and juggle."

On the great day, Encyclopedia and Sally went to the civic auditorium to watch Fangs perform. As they entered the lobby, a tall woman narrowly missed bumping into Sally.

The woman wore a yellow dress and carried a yellow suitcase. She hurried on without a word.

The detectives looked around for Fangs. They found him bending over a water fountain.

"Thanks for coming," he said. "I can use the support."

"We'll clap like a family of seals," Encyclopedia said.

Sally gazed around at the other contestants. "Aren't you a bit young?" she asked Fangs. "Everyone else is a teen-ager."

"I don't expect to win today," Fangs said matter-of-factly. "I'm after experience. I want to go to college free."

"Roll that past us one more time," requested Encyclopedia.

"If I'm satisfied with my juggling today," Fangs said, "I'll work on it during the next seven years so I can get a scholarship."

"Colleges don't give scholarships for *juggling*," Sally protested.

"Boy, are you ever out of it," Fangs said. "These days colleges hand out scholarships for anything."

He lowered his voice. "Wait'll you see my secret act. I juggle three apples and take bites in midair. At the end I'm juggling three apple cores."

"Wow!" cried Encyclopedia. "That's *core*-dination!"

"The hard part is working with objects of unequal weight," Fangs said. "You have to use different force. But having a pair of front teeth like mine is an advantage."

"Switch to candy apples and you'll win a scholarship to Harvard or Yale," Sally said.

"I want to go to Oberlin," stated Fangs.

A man in a white sport jacket came onto the stage. He announced the start of tryouts.

"The acrobats are first," Fangs said. "Then come the dancers and jugglers. I'd better begin loosening up."

He excused himself and went into the cloakroom. The first pair of acrobats had completed their turn when he emerged. He was pale.

"M-my apples are gone," he stammered in disbelief. "I've searched everywhere. Somebody stole them!"

The detectives pressed him for more information. All he could tell them was that he had carried his apples into the auditorium in a small, dusty yellow suitcase that he'd found that morning in the attic. He had put the suitcase on a shelf in the cloakroom twenty minutes ago.

"A woman with a yellow suitcase left as we came into the auditorium," Sally said.

"Did the suitcase have a zipper?" asked Fangs.

Sally thought a moment. "No, it had clasps."

"Then it wasn't mine," Fangs said.

"Can't you get more apples?" inquired Encyclopedia.

"There isn't time," answered Fangs. His expression hardened. "Besides, I'd rather find the dirty thief. And when I do. . . ." His lip curled above his powerful front teeth.

"Button up," cautioned Encyclopedia. "How many other jugglers are in the tryouts?"

"Two," answered Fangs. "Archie Longmire and Claire Foss."

"Archie and Claire are afraid Fangs might outclass them," declared Sally. "They have the most to gain if he can't perform. Let's question them."

Encyclopedia was not nearly so eager as Sally to jump into the case. Archie Longmire was a warm and friendly tenth grader who juggled plates. Claire Foss was only thirteen, but she was sturdy, and as warm and friendly as an iceberg kissing an ocean liner. She juggled bowling balls.

Fangs spotted Archie and Claire standing together in a corner of the auditorium. Sally marched straight up to them.

"Fangs came here with his juggling equipment in a suitcase," she said. "Now the suitcase is missing."

"Gee, that's a shame," Archie said. "Will he be able to go on?"

"You know I won't!" blurted Fangs.

"I'm sorry," Archie said. "But I never saw him with a suitcase."

"Me, neither," said Claire. She scowled at Encyclopedia. "Are you *accusing* anyone?"

"No, no, no," replied Encyclopedia as fast as he was able. "We thought you might help us find the thief. Did you notice anyone leaving with a small suitcase?"

"Heck," said Archie. "Kids with suitcases and shopping bags have been coming and going all morning."

"Then we'll have to comb every inch of the building," Encyclopedia said heavily. "The suitcase is old and dusty, and the thief is certain to have left fingerprints."

"Wait a second," said Claire. "Now that I

think about it, I did see someone suspicious. A woman in a bright yellow dress was leaving in one big hurry as you came in. She had a suitcase!"

"I saw her, too," said Archie. "She was in an awful rush. She nearly bumped into Sally. And she had a yellow suitcase like Fangs's."

"That wasn't my suitcase," Fangs said. "Mine has a zipper."

Sally turned to Encyclopedia. "It'll take us a week to search all the rooms in the building," she said. "We're not even sure if the thief hid the suitcase or made off with it."

"Why don't you ask the thief?" suggested Encyclopedia.

WHO WAS THE THIEF?

(Turn to page 87 for the solution to "The Case of the Boy Juggler.")

THE CASE
OF THE
PRACTICAL
JOKERS

SUNDAY ENCYCLOPEDIA AND SALLY took the number 9 bus to the farmlands north of town to visit Lucy Fibbs. Lucy was training her pet hog, Julius Caesar, to be the strongest hog in the world.

As they got off the bus, the detectives saw Julius exercising. Lucy's poodle led the hog by a leash and was setting a fast pace along a cornfield.

"Roadwork builds up Julius's muscles," Lucy said after she had greeted the detectives. "I don't want him to be just bacon."

Sally whistled. "Who'd believe a little dog could run a big hog!"

"I've taught Julius to obey simple commands," Lucy said proudly. "I want him to be smart, too."

The poodle and Julius drew up beside Lucy. She patted both animals and undid the leash.

"Julius is only eight months old," she said. "I'm bringing him along slowly, but already he can pull seven tons."

"Wait till he reaches his full growth," Encyclopedia murmured.

"He'll pull fifteen tons easily," asserted Lucy. "He's tremendous—a once-in-a-lifetime hog."

She led the detectives up the dirt road toward the house. Julius trotted by his pal, the poodle, and oinked contentedly.

Three tall youths were on the side lawn. Encyclopedia recognized them: Conrad Benton, Morris Purvey, and Andrew Wagner. They were sons of neighboring farmers.

Lucy said, "They stop by to check on Julius. But one of them is *too* interested. I think he's the person who tried to steal Julius last night. He was scared off by the poodle's barking."

Suddenly she put a finger to her lips and

whispered, "They love practical jokes. Watch."

Conrad was lying on his back, apparently asleep. Morris was kneeling at Conrad's feet, tying his shoelaces together. Andrew had sneaked up behind Morris.

Andrew struck a match and lighted several other matches that he had planted between the sole and upper part of Morris's shoe. As Morris finished tying Conrad's laces together, the flames burned to the matchheads in his own shoe and flared.

Morris screamed, "Yikes!" and hopped in pain. Conrad, startled, leaped up, tried to take a step, and tumbled over his bound feet. Andrew roared with laughter.

"Morris will have some blister," observed Encyclopedia.

"I don't like practical jokes," Sally said disgustedly.

Morris did a one-legged turkey trot for several minutes before he tried his weight on the wounded foot.

"Why is Andrew's clothing wet?" asked Encyclopedia.

"I'll show you," Lucy answered and took the detectives to the rear of the house. The porch was puddled with water.

"I'm alone in the house today," Lucy said.

"A little while ago, Andrew came into the house and asked for a drink. While he was inside, either Morris or Conrad balanced a plastic bucket of water above the screen door."

"When Andrew came out, *kaplum!*" Sally said.

"He swore he'd get even," Lucy said. "The three boys don't like one another very much."

"What about the attempt to steal Julius last night?" asked Encyclopedia.

"I've laid a trap for the thief," Lucy replied. "I made up a record of Julius's diet in a little black book. This morning, I showed each boy where I keep it."

"Was that wise?" Sally asked.

"The book is a fake," Lucy said. "Julius will eat anything. I just give him a lot of it."

Encyclopedia smiled. "You expect the boy who failed to steal Julius to try to steal the book and develop a Hercules hog of his own."

"When he tries to snatch the book, I'll catch him!" said Lucy.

She walked into the living room to fetch the book and show it to the detectives. It was gone!

"The thief must have sneaked in while I answered the telephone a few minutes before you arrived."

Encyclopedia went looking for clues. On the bare hall floor he found a faint set of wet footprints. They led from the rear door to the carpet of the living room and back.

"Crazy!" exclaimed Sally. "They look like the thief walked in mittens!"

"His socks had holes through which his big toes stuck out," Encyclopedia explained.

"He must have taken off his shoes on the wet porch so as not to make any noise," Lucy said.

"All we have to do is search each boy and find the book and two naked toes," Sally declared.

"Suppose they won't let us?" asked Lucy.

"You're right, they're too big," Sally replied. "So . . . we'll just have to be sure of our man first."

"The thief might be Andrew," Lucy said.

"Right," Sally said. "There's something wrong with his story about getting soaked by the bucket. How did he keep his matches dry enough to give Morris a hot foot?"

"Sorry," Lucy said, "I have to tell you that he borrowed the matches from me *after* he got soaked."

"That makes Morris our man," Sally said, though hesitantly. "Look how quietly he sneaked up on Conrad. He's light-fingered, too. He tied Conrad's shoelaces together without waking him."

"Maybe Conrad wasn't really asleep," Lucy pointed out. "He could have been acting to make us believe he'd been sleeping when the book was stolen."

Sally grunted helplessly. "This case beats me. What do you think, Encyclopedia?"

"I think," said the detective, "that we can safely accuse—"

WHOM?

(Turn to page 88 for the solution to "The Case of the Practical Jokers.")

THE CASE OF THE MARATHON RUNNER

CICERO STURGESS, IDAVILLE'S GREAT-est child actor, staggered into the Brown Detective Agency and fell on his face.

Encyclopedia and Sally rushed to his side. As they stooped to aid him, Cicero jumped up and grinned.

"I fooled you!" he cried.

"You're not hurt?" Sally said. "What's the big idea?"

"The marathon race tomorrow," Cicero answered. "It will launch my stage career nationwide. Think of the publicity! 'Ten-Year-Old Actor Proves His Grit!' "

Sally gasped in astonishment. "You've entered the Idaville marathon?"

"Every step," Cicero replied. "When I collapse at the finish line, I'll be the center of attention."

He went into his finish-line act again, lurching like a man dying of the bends.

"There'll be waves of interviews," he said, straightening. "You know, radio, television, newspapers. I'll feed 'em a few choice lines about the conquest of pain and how I never quit. Then I'll bring up my acting career."

"Why should anyone interview you?" inquired Sally. "How can you hope to win?"

"Who said anything about winning?" asked Cicero.

"Well, what—"

"I've been training for three days," declared Cicero. "Plenty of overeating and no exercise. I'm in shape, and I'm ready. I plan to finish last."

Encyclopedia wished him luck.

"I'll need it," replied Cicero. "Anyone can win a marathon. It isn't so easy to finish last."

With that, he departed the way he had entered, staggering toward an imaginary finish line.

The next day, Sunday, the detectives biked to City Hall, where the marathon was to begin. Cicero, the youngest runner, wore number 84.

At two o'clock, the starter fired his gun. Encyclopedia and Sally watched till the runners were out of sight. Then they peddled to the seven-mile mark of the race.

Nearly two hours later, Cicero jogged by. He was locked in a struggle for last place with a woman wearing a neck brace and a man running backward.

"Keep it up, Cicero!" Sally shouted. To Encyclopedia she said with a sigh, "This may go on all night."

There was nothing to do but telephone their parents and say they would be home late. They went to a movie and ate dinner at Andy's Pizza Parlor.

Night had fallen when they stopped outside the Idaville Concert Hall, a mile from the finish, and cheered a few runners laboring past. Encyclopedia pointed to the large electric sign above the concert hall: "Tonight Only—Railroad Brotherhood Band Concert."

"We might as well go in," he said. "Cicero won't be coming by for another hour."

The detectives bought tickets and forgot about the time as they sat listening to the music. Just before the intermission, the band struck up a medley of state songs.

"This piece sounds like 'I've Been Workin' on the Railroad,' " Sally said. "But the program lists the title as 'Eyes of Texas.' "

"Both songs have the same tune," Encyclopedia explained, glancing down at Sally's program. He noticed her watch. It was nearly nine o'clock!

"We may miss Cicero!" he gasped. "C'mon!"

By taking a shortcut, they reached the finish line of the marathon in three minutes. The area was nearly deserted.

All the spectators had gone home, and the last officials were preparing to leave. The first-aid station had closed. A single reporter chatted idly with men from a television truck as they packed their gear.

Suddenly someone shouted, "Hold everything! Here comes one more!"

A TV man grabbed a camera and aimed it down the shadowed street at a small figure— number 84. It was Cicero! The young actor wobbled like a broken top and fell across the finish line.

"He's done it!" yelled Sally. "He's lost to everyone!"

"He took more than seven hours," marveled Encyclopedia.

Surrounded by a storm of congratulations, Cicero quickly livened to his task. He struck pose after pose, gestured, bowed, and likened the hardships of a marathon to getting ahead in acting.

He was delivering lines from his most recent dramatic appearance when Millicent Potter, number 76, crossed the finish line. All at once, Cicero was without an audience. Everyone dashed to welcome the new loser.

Millicent, a pretty tenth grader, seemed astonished by her sudden importance. She hadn't realized, she said, that she was the only runner still on the course.

"This is my first marathon, and I didn't think I could make it," she said, panting. "Then I passed the concert hall while the Railroad Band was playing 'Eyes of Texas.' The music inspired me."

She wiped her face with a forearm and smiled bravely at the TV camera.

"I started humming as I ran the last mile," she said. "Music gives me strength. Music is my life. I hope to be a singer after I graduate high school. But it's so hard for an unknown to get a break today. . . ."

Cicero was listening to her in shock. She had not only stolen his great moment, she was using it to advance *her* career.

"I feel sorry for Cicero," Sally said. "What tough luck to have outrun Millicent."

"He didn't," replied Encyclopedia. "When the officials learn what Millicent did, they'll declare Cicero the rightful last-place finisher."

WHAT DID ENCYCLOPEDIA MEAN?

(Turn to page 89 for the solution to "The Case of the Marathon Runner.")

Solution
THE CASE
OF THE
SUPERMARKET SHOPPER

Encyclopedia realized the thief was Mr. Houser, who made sure Mr. Quinn was away from his house a good while.

Mr. Quinn had to buy four rolls of paper towels, a whisk broom for Mr. Trad, and two loaves of bread for Mr. Finkelstein. With only seven purchases, Mr. Quinn could use the speed counter, where the limit was ten.

So Mr. Houser asked for four tubes of toothpaste to bring the total to *eleven* purchases. Therefore, Mr. Quinn had to wait in one of the long lines at the regular checkout counters, delaying his return home by fifteen or twenty minutes.

The painting was found hidden in Mr. Houser's attic.

Solution
THE CASE
OF THE
DINOSAUR HUNTER

Bugs said the towel had fallen into Mill Pond and that he had hung it out to dry. Because it was a plain white towel, he didn't think anyone could prove it wasn't his.

Wrong! Encyclopedia could.

The detective *felt* the towel. It was soft and fluffy.

Only a towel that has been machine dried—like Garth's was—will come out soft and fluffy. A towel that has been thoroughly soaked and hung out in the air will feel stiff after it has dried.

Thanks to Encyclopedia, Bugs took back the dinosaur license and returned Garth's towel.

THE CASE
OF THE
USED FIRECRACKERS

Bugs Meany blamed Encyclopedia and Sally for setting off firecrackers. Actually, he and his Tigers had been setting them off all summer.

Bugs thought he had everything figured out. Officer Friedman naturally would radio his position when he arrived on the scene. So he wouldn't be sure about hearing a firecracker go off, as Bugs said it had.

But Bugs had forgotten about the birds. If the detectives had really set off a firecracker, the noise would have frightened the birds away.

As Encyclopedia pointed out to Officer Friedman, the birds were sitting peacefully on the wires above them.

Solution
THE CASE
OF THE
UGLIEST DOG

Earl Hanes sought to improve his dog's chances of winning the ugliest-dog class.

While pretending to pat Twitchy, Earl secretly fed her sleeping pills. But then he became afraid that Scott Curtis had unknowingly photographed him in the act. So Earl removed the evidence, Scott's color film, and substituted a roll of his own, which was black and white.

Later, Kate Felton didn't wish to pose in her orange blouse and Sally's purple skirt. Impatient with Kate, Earl gave himself away. He shouted that the colors "won't show." Only the person who *knew* Scott had black-and-white film in his camera could have been so certain.

Because of Encyclopedia's keen ear and memory, Earl had to confess.

Solution
THE CASE
OF
HILBERT'S SONG

The thief was Maggie, who pretended to be terribly upset about the disappearance of the tape.

Using an eyedropper, she faked a tear. But she placed the drop of water on the outside corner of her eye. That was her mistake!

If only one tear falls, it will run from the *inside* corner of the eye, by the nose, and not from the *outside* corner.

Encyclopedia spotted the mistake, and Maggie confessed. She had hidden the tape, planning to sell it as her own.

Hilbert sent the tape to a record company. It was returned with a note saying his song had a pretty good beat, but it wasn't loud enough, and it needed more singers.

Solution
THE CASE
OF THE
CROWING ROOSTER

Encyclopedia noticed what the other children had overlooked—what really made the rooster crow. It wasn't the ray.

Bill had kept the rooster hidden under his overcoat, in darkness. When he took it out, the bird saw the first shades of *sunset.* But it thought, after being kept in darkness, that the time of day was *sunrise.*

Hence the rooster did what roosters do naturally at sunrise. It crowed.

Thanks to Encyclopedia, none of the children gave Wilford money for the phony ray.

Solution
THE CASE
OF THE
BUBBLE GUM SHOOTOUT

Teresa wasn't the "perfect stranger" Malcolm made her out to be. She had come *prepared* to blow bubble gum.

Encyclopedia realized immediately that the peanut butter wasn't her lunch, as she pretended. There was nothing to spread it on or eat it with.

What was the peanut butter for? Encyclopedia knew.

Peanut butter is the handiest thing to use for *untangling hair stuck with bubble gum.*

After being faced with the evidence, Malcolm admitted he had cheated. Teresa was his cousin—the under-sixteen girls' bubble gum champion of nearby Glenn City.

Cephas lost the shootout, but he won the bike.

Solution
THE CASE
OF THE
BOY JUGGLER

The thief was Archie, who wanted to win the juggling contest.

When Encyclopedia remarked that the thief's fingerprints would be on Fangs's suitcase, Archie became frightened. He tried to cast suspicion on the woman in the yellow dress. He said, ". . . she had a yellow suitcase like Fangs's."

But earlier Archie had said he hadn't seen Fangs's suitcase. So he couldn't have known it was yellow unless he was the thief!

Foiled by his own words, he showed Fangs where he'd hidden the suitcase.

Fangs had just enough time to take the stage. But without a warm-up, he gagged on an apple and had to withdraw.

Solution
THE CASE
OF THE
PRACTICAL JOKERS

Conrad had put the water bucket over the screen door, but Morris was the thief.

Having failed to kidnap Julius the night before, he stole the book. He expected to grow his own super-strong hog by learning what to feed it.

Encyclopedia knew because Morris hopped around "for several minutes" after receiving the "hot foot." An innocent boy would have removed the painfully hot shoe immediately.

Morris was afraid to take off his shoe and show the telltale hole in his sock, Encyclopedia realized.

After Conrad and Andrew threatened to hold him down and search him, Morris confessed.

Solution
THE CASE
OF THE
MARATHON RUNNER

Millicent lied when she said she had "passed the concert hall while the Railroad Band was playing 'Eyes of Texas.' "

She knew the sign out front gave the name of the band. So, running past, she would have assumed the song was "I've Been Workin' on the Railroad."

Only if she had been *inside* the hall and seen the program could she have known the song was "Eyes of Texas." Both songs, as Encyclopedia told Sally, have the same tune!

Thanks to Encyclopedia, the truth came out. She had left the race after two miles and had not come back until the last mile.

Millicent was disqualified. Cicero was declared the official loser.

Cushing Public Library

8 1789 00703333 5

DATE DUE

WITHDRAWN

CUSHING LIBRARY
PO Box 25
Cushing, ME 04563

HIGHSMITH 45-220